DON'T HURT ME, MAMA

Muriel Stanek

pictures by Helen Cogancherry

Albert Whitman & Company, Niles, Illinois

Library of Congress Cataloging in Publication Data

Stanek, Muriel.
Don't hurt me, Mama.

Summary: A kind and sensitive school nurse sees
that a young victim of child abuse and her abusing
mother get help.
[1. Child abuse—Fiction]   I. Cogancherry, Helen,
ill.   II. Title.
PZ7.S78637Do   1983   [E]   83-16771
ISBN 0-8075-1689-9

Text © 1983 by Muriel Stanek
Illustrations © 1983 by Helen Cogancherry
Published in 1983 by Albert Whitman & Company, Niles, Illinois
Published simultaneously in Canada
by General Publishing, Limited, Toronto
All rights reserved. Printed in U.S.A.

12 11 10 9 8 7 6 5 4 3 2

Dedicated to all the people who work with
abused children and their families.
M.S.

To all children, whose
innocence and dignity must be preserved.
H.C.

Mama and I live together,
just the two of us.
We don't have anyone else.

Last September, my daddy left us.
And we haven't heard from him since.

Mama and I didn't have enough money
to stay in our house.
We had to move to a small apartment
in the city, where no one knew us.

Before we moved, Mama and I used to
go to church.
Everybody sang songs together.
And we learned about being good to
one another.

Afterward, we ate homemade cakes
and drank lemonade.
When it was time to go home,
people shook hands with us and
asked us to come again.
I felt safe and happy.

But after Daddy left, we didn't go out anymore.

Mama cried a lot.
She said nobody cared about her.

"I care about you, Mama," I told her.
"I care."

But she wouldn't listen.

Mama couldn't find a job.
And sometimes she drank too much.
Then she got mean and hit me,
even when I wasn't bad.

After a while, when Mama got like that,
I went to my room,
where she couldn't see me.

I felt scared and lonely.
I didn't know what to do.

One day when I came home from school,
Mama wasn't there.
I looked everywhere,
but I couldn't find her.

I went outside.
An old woman stopped to talk to me.
"I'm Sarah Hawkins, and this is
my dog, Sam," she said.
"We live upstairs.
Come visit, anytime you want.
Bring your mother, too."

"Okay," I told her.

It was getting dark now, so I went inside.
Mama still wasn't home.
After a long time, I saw someone slowly
walking down the street.
It was Mama.

I ran and opened the door.
"Where were you, Mama?" I asked.
But she didn't answer.

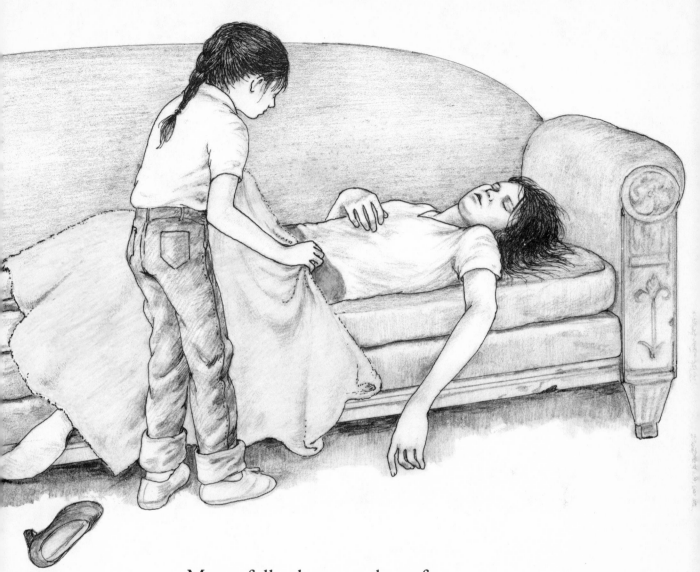

Mama fell asleep on the sofa.
I covered her with a blanket
and went to bed without any supper.

In the morning, Mama was sitting
at the kitchen table.

"I'm hungry, Mama," I said.

"Get your own breakfast," she
answered.

But when I tried to pour the milk,
it spilled all over.

"You can't do anything right," she yelled,
"just like your good-for-nothing father,
wherever he is."

Mama grabbed a belt and hit me hard.
I covered my face with my arms.
"Don't hurt me, Mama," I cried.

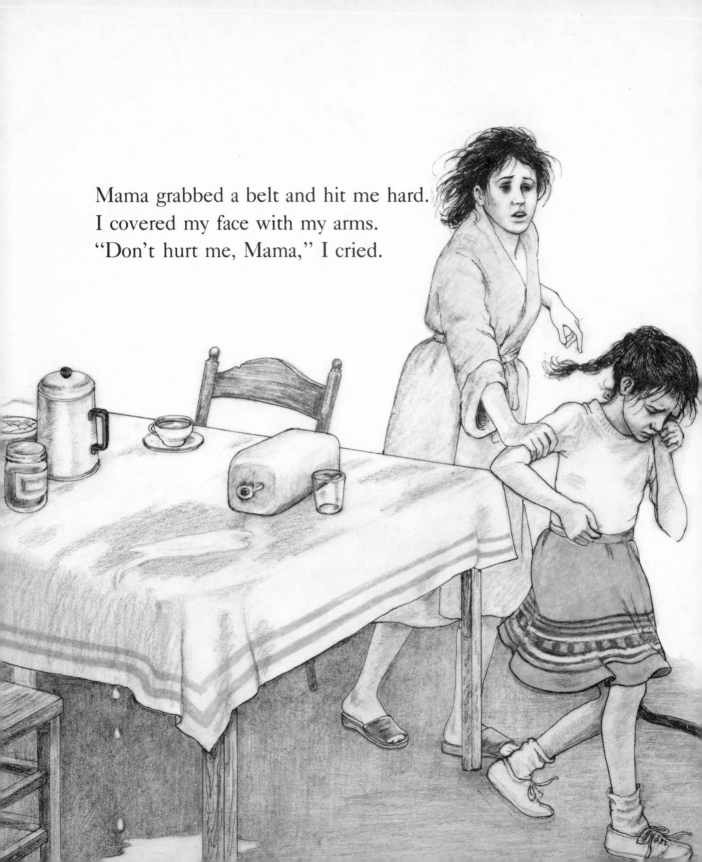

"I didn't mean it," Mama said. "I didn't
mean it."

She tried to hug me, but I pulled away.

"Don't tell anyone," she said
as I left for school.

"Are you okay?" my teacher asked.
I didn't answer.
"The school nurse should see you," he said.
And he took me to her office.

"How did this happen?" asked the nurse
when she saw the marks on my legs and arms.

I didn't tell.

"Did someone beat you?" she whispered.
"Was it your mother?"

I didn't want to cry, but I couldn't
help it.

"I wasn't bad," I said, "but Mama
hit me anyway."

"It isn't your fault," the nurse said.
"Your mother has problems that are
too much for her to handle alone.
Maybe we can find a way to help her.
I'll do something about it today."

Then the nurse took me to
the lunchroom for breakfast.
She was nice, I thought.
Maybe I could talk
to her again.

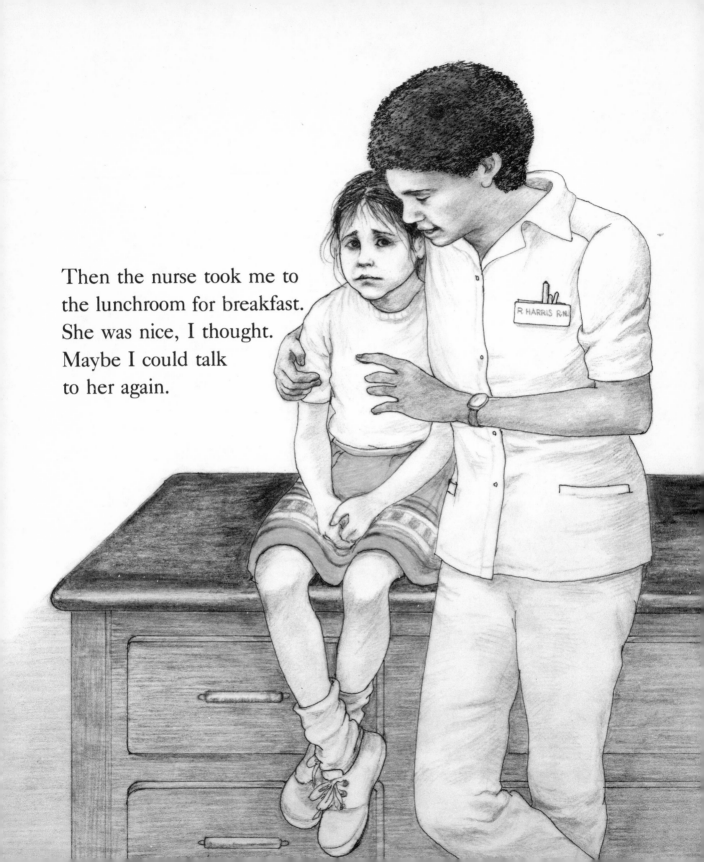

Mama was waiting for me after school.
She put her arms around me and said,
"Forgive me, darling."

I hugged her hard.

Mama told me a social worker had been
to see her.
They had gone to the community health
center together.

"Lots of people with problems go there,"
Mama said. "The social worker will try
to help me find a job. Then I won't be
so sad and angry, and I can take better
care of you."

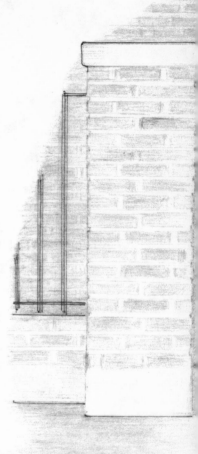

Now Mama goes to the community center
every week.
She meets with other people who have
problems.
She says they help one another.
I stay with Mrs. Hawkins and Sam
while she's gone.

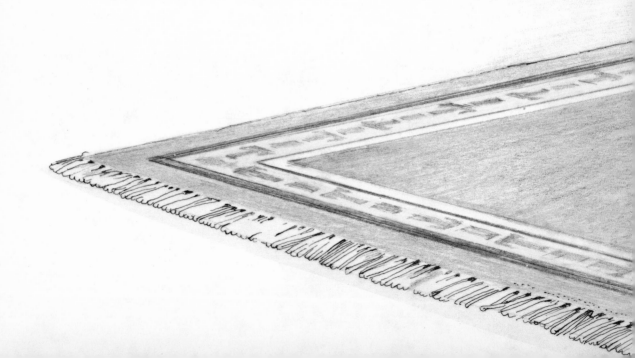

I think Mama is feeling better.
She hasn't hit me for a long time.
Today I said, "Let's go to church again,
Mama. Church always makes us feel happy."

"That's a good idea," she answered.
"I'll buy you a new hair ribbon to wear."

We love each other,
Mama and me.